3 1994 01378 6279

SANTA ANA PUBLIC LIBRARY
NEWHOPE BRANCH

D0603946

AR PTS: 0.5

J FICTION QUANTZ, D.
Quantz, Daniel SUPERHEROES QUAN
Spider-Man in Duel to the death with the vulture!
$21.35
NEW HOPE 31994013786279

VISIT US AT

www.abdopub.com

Spotlight, a division of ABDO Publishing Company Inc., is the school and library distributor of the Marvel Entertainment books.

Library bound edition © 2006

MARVEL, and all related character names and the distinctive likenesses thereof are trademarks of Marvel Characters, Inc., and is/are used with permission. Copyright © 2005 Marvel Characters, Inc. All rights reserved. www.marvel.com

MARVEL, Spider-Man: TM & © 2005 Marvel Characters, Inc. All rights reserved. www.marvel.com. This book is produced under license from Marvel Characters, Inc.

Library of Congress Cataloging-in-Publication Data

Duel to the death with the vulture

ISBN 1-59961-012-4 (Reinforced Library Bound Edition)

All Spotlight books are reinforced library binding
and manufactured in the United States of America

NEW YORKERS ARE ACCUSTOMED TO WATCHING THEIR BACKS...
BUT LATELY, DANGER COMES FROM A NEW DIRECTION...
HEY!!! GIVE THAT BACK, YOU THIEF!!!
FROM ABOVE.
ONE WAY
ONE WAY
DAILY BUGLE
April 12th, 2004
THREAT FROM ABOVE!
The Voracious Vulture Strikes Again!
REWARD: $500 paid for QUALITY Pic
of the Vulture OR Spider-

Queens, NY.
HEY!!! COME BACK HERE!!!
COME ON, FLASH! GIVE IT BACK!!
SHWOOMP
GREAT PLAY, FLASH!
YEAH, LET'S HOPE IT WORKS TONIGHT AGAINST THE TIGERS.
THEY'LL BE A LOT TOUGHER THAN PUNY PETER PARKER HERE, BUT NOT NEARLY AS MUCH FUN!
WHAT'S THIS?! WHO'S THE VULTURE?!
PERFECT, AND HERE I HAVE NO CHANGE...

EXCUSE ME... DO EITHER OF YOU HAVE ANY CHANGE? QUARTERS?
ANYONE?

I NEVER THOUGHT IT'D BE SO HARD TO GET TWO LOUSY QUARTERS--
HI, AUNT MAY... WHAT WAS OUR LANDLORD DOING HERE?
HELLO, PETER, WHY DON'T YOU COME IN AND HAVE A SEAT. I NEED TO TALK TO YOU ABOUT SOMETHING.
PETER, MONEY HAS BEEN VERY TIGHT AND I'VE BEEN UNABLE TO KEEP UP ON THE RENT.
NO WAY! WE CAN'T LOSE THE HOUSE!
DEAR, WITHOUT UNCLE BEN'S INCOME WE MAY NOT HAVE A CHOICE.
NO! I'LL QUIT SCHOOL AND GET A JOB... ANYTHING...
YOU WILL DO NO SUCH THING!
PETER, YOU ARE DESTINED FOR GREAT THINGS... I WILL NOT LET YOU TRADE IN YOUR FUTURE FOR A LITTLE BIT OF RENT MONEY.
BUT WHAT ARE WE GONNA DO?!
I DON'T KNOW YET.
I CAN'T BELIEVE THIS! THERE'S GOT TO BE SOMETHING--
HANG ON...
THREAT
The Voracious Vu
REWARD: $500 paid for QUALITY Pictures of the V OR Spider-man
AUNT MAY, DIDN'T UNCLE BEN HAVE A CAMERA?

HERE IT IS. I'M SURE YOUR UNCLE BEN WOULD HAVE WANTED YOU TO HAVE THIS.
THANKS! THIS LITTLE GADGET MIGHT JUST HELP US PAY THE BILLS.
OH, NO... DON'T SELL IT!
NO, DON'T WORRY. I'VE GOT A BETTER IDEA.
Later.
I'M SURE I COULD TAKE BETTER PICTURES THAN ANYONE OF THIS VULTURE CHARACTER.
NO ONE GETS AS CLOSE TO THE ACTION AS SPIDER-MAN!
THIS SHOULD BE HIGH ENOUGH TO SEE EVERYTHING.
NOW... WHERE WOULD HE BE TODAY?

THAT'S STRANGE--
ALL RIGHT!! THOSE ARE GONNA BE GREAT SHOTS!!!
I GOTTA ADMIT, THIS WAS A BRILLIANT IDEA--

WELL, WELL, WELL...THE "AMAZING" SPIDER-MAN, EH?
OR IS IT, THE "SPECTACULAR" SPIDER-MAN?
I THINK I PREFER... THE "INSUBSTANTIAL" SPIDER-MAN.
OR MAYBE, THE "UNGUARDED" SPIDER-MAN.
OR MAYBE JUST...
THE "OVERRATED"...

WHAT THE--? WHERE?! WHAT JUST HAPPENED?!
FZZZZ
OH, GREAT, I'M ALL OUT OF WEB FLUID...
...AND THESE WALLS ARE TOO SLIPPERY TO CLIMB.
OK, GENIUS, YOU GOT YOURSELF IN HERE. HOW THE HECK ARE YOU GETTING OUT?
WELL... I DO HAVE ONE LAST TRICK IN THE BAG...
SPOK
AAARRRGH!!!

Some super hero...
I just got my
tail whooped
by an old man.
At least these photos
should turn out
good... For what I
just went through,
they BETTER!
That feeling I got before
the Vulture attacked...
there was something
strange about it...
DARK
ROOM
23
It was different
than the normal
warning sense I get.
Almost like those
electro-magnetic
spheres they had
at the science fair...
THAT'S IT!
Electro-magnetism!
That's what ruined
this picture where he
flew right over me...
That's GOT to be
what makes him fly!

Daily Bugle.
ILY BUGLE
CAN I HELP YOU?
YEAH, HI. I, UM, I HAVE SOME PICTURES I'D LIKE TO SELL MR. JAMESON.
UH HUH, I'LL HAVE TO LOOK AT THEM FIRST. MR. JAMESON'S A VERY BUSY MAN.
I THINK THEY'RE TERRIFIC, SIR!
YEAH? HMM... I GUESS THEY'RE NOT SO BAD...

I'LL GIVE YOU A HUNDRED BUCKS FOR THE LOT OF 'EM.

A HUNDRED BUCKS? NO THANKS.
I'LL JUST TAKE THEM OVER TO *THE TIMES*...

ALRIGHT, KID, I'LL GIVE YOU FIVE HUNDRED.
BUT I WANT FIRST LOOK ON EVERYTHING ELSE!

THANKS FOR YOUR HELP IN THERE.
I, UH... I'M SORRY I DIDN'T CATCH YOUR NAME.
BETTY.
HI BETTY, I'M PETER PARKER. AND I'M A PHOTOGRAPHER.
Later in Peter's Basement.
If the Vulture really uses electro-magnetism to fly, then this little beauty should be just what I need.
And with all these extra web-fluid cartridges, I should never run out again.
Now, where is that little buzzard?

EXCHANGE
PARK
That evening.
CHIEF! WE'RE ALL SET! SNIPERS ARE IN POSITION.
S.W.A.T.
GOOD. I WANT THEM READY TO FIRE IF THE VULTURE GETS ANYWHERE CLOSE.
WHAT MAKES YOU SO SURE HE'S COMING?
DON'T KNOW FOR SURE, BUT WE GOT THIS.
TRUCK'S COMING!
I shall steal the diamond shipment from under your noses!
Yours Truly, The Vulture
I'LL TAKE THOSE!
Police
NO!!!

THIS IS IT! I'M RICH! I'LL NEVER HAVE TO STEAL AGAIN!
OF COURSE, IF YOU'RE GOOD AT SOMETHING, WHY QUIT?
There he is! I'd know that shade of PUKE green from a mile away!
NOT EVEN A SINGLE HELICOPTER! UNBELIEVABLE! I'M HOME FREE!

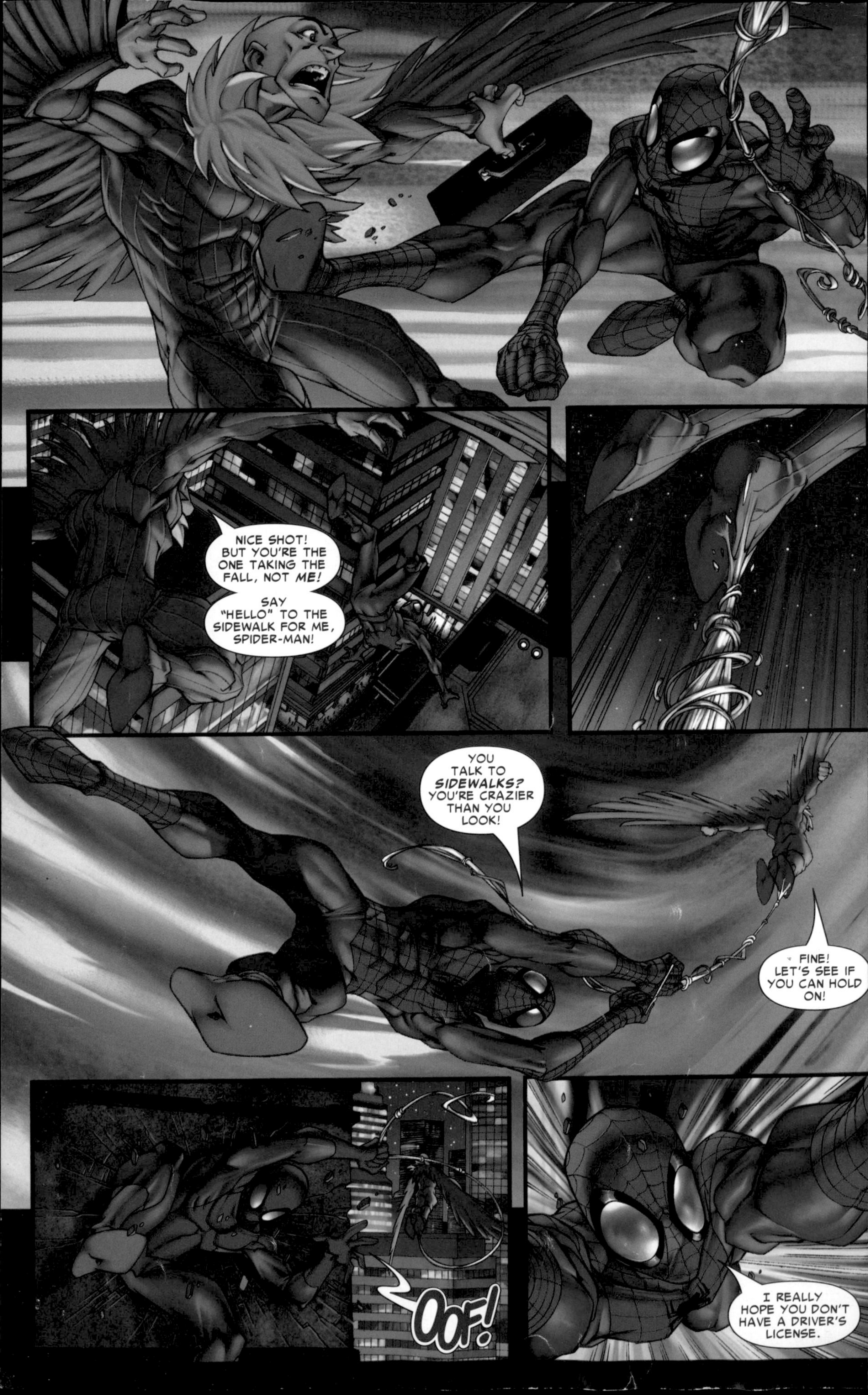
NICE SHOT! BUT YOU'RE THE ONE TAKING THE FALL, NOT *ME!*
SAY "HELLO" TO THE SIDEWALK FOR ME, SPIDER-MAN!
YOU TALK TO *SIDEWALKS?* YOU'RE CRAZIER THAN YOU LOOK!
FINE! LET'S SEE IF YOU CAN HOLD ON!
OOF!
I REALLY HOPE YOU DON'T HAVE A DRIVER'S LICENSE.

HEY! LET GO!
SILLY OLD MAN, DIDN'T ANYONE EVER TELL YOU?
TURKEYS CAN'T FLY!
I'M FALLING!! THIS ISN'T POSSIBLE!!!
YOUR WINGS MAY BE CLIPPED, BUT THAT GARBAGE BIN SHOULD OFFER YOU AN EQUALLY SOFT LANDING... AND GIVE THE POLICE A CHANCE TO PICK UP THE TRASH!

THE POLICE WERE READY AND WAITING FOR THE VULTURE AS HE ENDED UP RIGHT WHERE HE BELONGED—IN THE GARBAGE.
BUT SPIDER-MAN'S SENSES BEGAN TO FLAIR UP...
BECAUSE ON THE OTHER SIDE OF TOWN A MADMAN WAS TINKERING WITH A DEVICE THAT COULD THREATEN THE WHOLE WORLD!

JUST A HARMLESS OLD MAN, RIGHT?
WELL, THAT'S EXACTLY WHAT HE WANTS YOU TO THINK!
THIS THREAT TO OUR VERY HUMANITY HAS MORE UP HIS SLEEVE THAN JUST LIVER-SPOTS...

Midtown High School.
LOOK AT PETER PARKER BACK THERE. CLASS IS OVER AND HE CAN'T TEAR HIMSELF AWAY.
FLASH, BE NICE. HE'S PROBABLY ON THE VERGE OF SOME GREAT DISCOVERY.
LIKE WHAT, A SOCIAL LIFE?
MR. WARREN, DO YOU HAVE A MINUTE?
I ALWAYS HAVE A MINUTE FOR MY STAR PUPIL, WHAT'S UP?
I WANTED TO SHOW YOU SOMETHING I MADE THE OTHER DAY...
IT'S A KIND OF ANTI-MAGNETIC INVERTER-REVERSAL KIND OF DEAL...
A WHAT?! I'VE NEVER HEARD OF SUCH A THING.
I KNOW. I INVENTED IT. I'M THINKING OF CALLING IT THE PARKERIZER...
SO WHAT DOES IT DO?
HERE, LET ME SHOW YOU...
ZZZIIPPZZZ
ONE WEEK LATER...
OK, so I didn't know the Parkerizer would ERASE Mr. Warren's entire hard drive... guess picking the computer up for him from the repair shop is the LEAST I can do.
The Tinkerer Repair Shop
We Fix ALL Electronics
TVs, Microwaves, Computers-
CHEAP

YEAH, HI. ARE YOU MR. TINKERER? I'M HERE TO PICK UP A COMPUTER.
YES, MY BOY, I AM. COME IN. DO YOU HAVE THE CLAIM TAG?
AH! YOU'RE PICKING UP FOR MR. WARREN, THE SCIENCE TEACHER!
YEAH, THAT'S RIGHT. HOW DO YOU KNOW--?
I'LL BE RIGHT BACK.
MR. WARREN IS AN IMPORTANT MAN... HIS WAS ONE OF THE SPECIAL JOBS.
DO YOU HAVE THAT COMPUTER READY FOR THE SCIENCE TEACHER, MY MINIONS?
IT IS READY, SIR.

THANKS FOR GOING TO GET THIS FOR ME, PETER.
IT'S THE LEAST I COULD-- WHOA! THE BACK JUST CAME OFF!
WHAT IN THE WORLD IS THIS?! SOMETHING'S NOT RIGHT HERE.
"MR. WARREN, I'VE GOT TO GO TAKE CARE OF SOMETHING..."
That was some kind of spying device... it's time I find out what this Tinkerer is up to...
Now, where is he?
Must be down here.
WHAT THE--?!

I TAKE IT YOU'RE NOT THE "WE COME IN PEACE"-TYPE ALIENS!
SO WHICH PLANET ARE YOU GUYS FROM?
THWAP!
WEAKLING?
LOSER?
HOW ABOUT FINISHED?
THAT'S ENOUGH.

HOW DO YOU LIKE MY MIND SCRAMBLER?
AAARRGH!! GREAT, YOU'VE INVENTED A GUN THAT GIVES PEOPLE MIGRAINES...
SELL IT TO AN ASPIRIN COMPANY, YOU'LL MAKE A FORTUNE!
OH, NO, YOU DON'T!
WHAT? WHERE'D HE GO?
AND IS THAT WHAT I THINK IT IS?
SO LONG, SPIDER-MAN. PERHAPS WE'LL MEET AGAIN, IN THE NEXT WORLD.
SO, HE WASN'T EVEN HUMAN AFTER ALL?!
I'M TELLING YOU GUYS, I SAW A UFO! IT WAS JUST LIKE THEY DESCRIBE-- ROUND AND SILVER--
NO WAY, MAN, YOU'RE LOSIN' IT.
I WONDER IF THE TINKERER AND HIS ALIEN MINIONS WERE COMING TO TAKE FLASH BACK HOME. BECAUSE ONE THING'S FOR SURE...
THERE IS NO INTELLIGENT LIFE IN OUTER SPACE.
End.